I0663201

The Screaming Skull

*A Haunted Tale of Murder, Madness,
and a Skull That Won't Stay Silent*

A Modern Translation

Adapted for the Contemporary Reader

F. Marion Crawford

Translated by Tim Zengerink

Table of Contents

Preface - Message to the Reader

What If You Could Help Rebuild the Greatest Library in Human History?

Thousands of years ago, the Library of Alexandria stood as the crown jewel of human achievement — a sanctuary where the collected wisdom of every known civilization was gathered, preserved, and shared freely.

And then, it was lost.

Through fire, conquest, and the slow erosion of time, humanity lost not just books — but ideas, dreams, discoveries, and stories that could have changed the world forever.

Today, the Library of Alexandria lives again — and you are invited to be a part of its restoration.

Our mission is simple yet profound:

To rebuild the greatest library the world has ever known, and to translate all timeless works into every language and dialect, so that no seeker of knowledge is ever left behind again.

By joining our movement to rebuild the modern Library of Alexandria, you become part of an unprecedented mission:

- **Unlimited Access to the Greatest Audiobooks & eBooks Ever Written:**

  Instantly explore thousands of legendary works—Plato, Shakespeare, Jane Austen, Leo Tolstoy, and countless more. All instantly available to read or listen, placing a complete literary universe at your fingertips.

- **Beautiful Paperback & Deluxe Editions at Printing Cost**

  Own any title as an elegant paperback, deluxe hardcover, or stunning collectible boxset—offered to you at true printing cost, delivered straight to your door. Build your personal Library of Alexandria, crafted for beauty, built for durability, and worthy of proud display.

- **Fresh Translations for Modern Readers—in Every Language & Dialect**

  Enjoy timeless masterpieces reimagined in clear, contemporary language—no more outdated phrases or obscure references. Alongside the original versions, we're tirelessly translating these classics into every language and dialect imaginable, ensuring accessibility and understanding across cultures and generations.

- **Join a Global Renaissance of Literature & Knowledge**

  You directly support expanding our library, publishing deluxe editions at true cost, translating works into all global languages, and bringing humanity's greatest stories to people everywhere. By joining today, you're not just preserving a legacy of masterpieces; you set in motion a powerful wave of literary accessibility.

Become a Torchbearer of Knowledge.

Join us for free now at **LibraryofAlexandria.com**

Together, we will ensure that the light of human wisdom never fades again.

With gratitude and a shared love of knowledge,

The Modern Library of Alexandria Team

Visit:

www.libraryofalexandria.com

Or scan the code below:

Introduction

Guilt, Retribution,
and the Voice of a Buried Truth

F. Marion Crawford's The Screaming Skull, first published in 1908, remains one of the most unnerving and atmospherically taut ghost stories ever written in the English language. The story centers not on elaborate hauntings or gruesome apparitions, but on a single object imbued with unbearable weight: a human skull that screams. Simple in structure but rich in psychological complexity, The Screaming Skull explores timeless themes of guilt, retribution, and the idea that the past—when suppressed or dishonored—never truly dies. In this short but unforgettable tale, Crawford constructs a masterclass in slow-burning horror, where the line between supernatural disturbance and personal conscience erodes with every word.

F. Marion Crawford was already well-known in his time as a novelist of historical fiction and romance, but it was in his supernatural stories—particularly those dealing with retribution beyond the grave—that he found his most enduring voice. Unlike writers who leaned into baroque Gothic theatrics, Crawford preferred an almost conversational delivery, grounding his tales in realism before drawing readers toward a creeping, inescapable horror. The Screaming Skull exemplifies this approach: a solitary narrator, a stormy night, a hearthside confession, and the eerie presence of a skull that may be screaming out of supernatural torment—or as a projection of repressed guilt.

What makes The Screaming Skull so psychologically compelling is the narrator himself: an aging sea captain named Braddock, who lives alone in a house that once belonged to his late friend and fellow seaman, Doctor Pratt. Pratt's wife had died under suspicious circumstances—circumstances that the reader quickly learns are not only relevant, but essential to the source of the haunting. The story is framed as Braddock's direct monologue to the reader, as he attempts to convince us that he's not insane, even as the events he recounts become more disturbing, more obsessive, and more tightly bound to the skull that he cannot get rid of.

This introduction will explore The Screaming Skull in its historical, literary, and thematic depth. We will examine how Crawford skillfully layers guilt, denial, social propriety, and superstition into a deeply psychological portrait of haunting. It is a story not just about the supernatural, but about the terror of the conscience—the way the mind, when burdened by complicity or cowardice, will summon its own ghosts to deliver justice. It is also a story that questions the limits of rationality, the moral consequences of silence, and the enduring human fear of what lies beneath the surface.

The Skull as Symbol: Object, Witness, and Voice

The titular skull in The Screaming Skull is more than a morbid relic—it is the story's emotional and symbolic anchor. A silent remnant of a once-living woman, it becomes the vessel through which the past makes its demands on the present. Crawford never gives the skull agency in the conventional sense; it does not float, glow, or actively attack. Instead, it occupies space. It returns when discarded. It emits a scream that no one else hears, except for Braddock—its sole caretaker, and perhaps, its last confessor.

From the beginning, Braddock insists that he did not kill Mrs. Pratt. He maintains that he only inherited the skull after his friend's mysterious death, but as his narrative unfolds, cracks begin to show in his certainty. He recounts how Mrs. Pratt had long been suspected of having died violently, possibly at the hands of her husband. Her death was sudden and unexplained, but covered up by the official story of natural causes. Rumors, of course, lingered. And so did her skull.

It is precisely this refusal to acknowledge the truth—to speak what everyone suspects but no one dares to say—that gives the skull its power. Crawford presents the skull as both literal and symbolic: it is the remains of a victim, yes, but it is also the embodiment of a truth that will not rest. The scream that echoes through Braddock's house is not merely supernatural—it is moral. It is the voice of injustice. Of complicity. Of a conscience that, once activated, cannot be silenced by rational explanation or superstition.

What Braddock fears most is not that the skull is haunted, but that the skull is right. That Mrs. Pratt was murdered. That Dr. Pratt got away with it. That Braddock himself—through silence, inaction, or cowardice—helped that injustice stand. The skull, then, is not just a ghostly relic; it is a mirror. A judge. An eternal reminder that the past cannot be buried, especially when it has not been spoken aloud.

Crawford's brilliance lies in never having to show the skull moving or acting beyond what Braddock reports. The terror is entirely in the narration—in

Braddock's increasing defensiveness, his insistence on rationality, and the way he circles around the unspoken guilt that underpins the entire story. The skull may scream, or it may not. But what is certain is that Braddock hears it. And what he hears is not the supernatural—it is his own conscience breaking through.

Isolation, Denial, and the Ghosts of the Unconfessed

Braddock's voice is at once rational and disturbed. He insists he is not afraid. He claims to be above superstition. And yet, he lives alone in a house with locked windows and doors, always anticipating the return of the skull that won't stay buried. The story takes place entirely within the domestic sphere—there are no priests, detectives, or villagers to mediate the haunting. There is only Braddock and his listener (the reader), locked in a space filled with suppressed emotion and unvoiced confession.

This framing device—of a man telling his own story while protesting his sanity—is a classic Gothic trope, but Crawford reinvents it with modern psychological depth. Braddock is not unreliable in the traditional sense. He is lucid, educated, and self-aware. What makes him unreliable is his denial. He cannot admit the truth to himself, much less to us. And so, the narrative becomes a spiral of self-justification. He tries to downplay the horror, to laugh it off, even as the events he describes grow darker and more disconcerting.

The story suggests that Braddock may have known more about Mrs. Pratt's death than he admits. He was close to the family. He likely suspected—or even witnessed—abuse. But he said nothing. Did nothing. And now, after all those years, the consequences have returned—not in the form of police or retribution, but in the form of a skull that will not be silenced. This is what makes The Screaming Skull so devastating. It is not about punishment in the legal sense. It is about spiritual justice. Moral debt. And the horror of knowing that silence can kill just as surely as action.

The story can also be read as an allegory for social respectability and repression. In Braddock's world, propriety is paramount. Appearances must be maintained. Gossip must be controlled. Crimes must be dressed in euphemism and buried under layers of civility. But beneath this polished surface lies a festering truth. The skull represents everything that polite society has tried to suppress—violence, betrayal, guilt—and its scream is the sound of that repression breaking through.

Even the setting reinforces this claustrophobia. The house is isolated. The storm outside rages. The narrator speaks to a silent guest who never responds. The effect is one of eerie intimacy. We are not watching a haunting—we are inside one. We are not reading about a confession—we are being made complicit in one.

Crawford's control of tone, pacing, and suggestion allows him to do what the best horror writers achieve: create a story that gets under the skin not through spectacle, but through suggestion. He makes the reader wonder not only whether the skull is haunted, but whether guilt itself can become a kind of haunting. Can a conscience, long ignored, become its own ghost?

That is the terrifying proposition at the heart of The Screaming Skull—and it is what makes the story endure.

The Enduring Power of Subtle Horror

F. Marion Crawford's contribution to supernatural literature is often understated, but in The Screaming Skull, we see the full force of his narrative genius. With minimal elements—a narrator, a skull, a single room— he conjures an atmosphere of suffocating dread and moral ambiguity. His story does not end with a climactic confrontation or a neatly resolved mystery. Instead, it leaves us with questions: What is the price of silence?

What does justice look like when no one speaks? And how loudly does the past scream when we try to bury it?

The Screaming Skull stands alongside the greatest tales of psychological horror—not because of how much it shows, but because of how much it suggests. Like Poe's "The Tell-Tale Heart" or James's "The Turn of the Screw," it reveals how the deepest horror lies not in the supernatural, but in the human mind. In our guilt. Our repression. Our fear of being found out—not by others, but by ourselves.

Today, in a world where moral complicity and social silence are still urgent issues, Crawford's story feels eerily relevant. The skull still screams—not just in haunted houses, but in history books, courtrooms, and the darkened chambers of the soul. And as readers, we must ask what we would hear in its cry—if we, too, were left alone in the dark, with nothing but the voice of our own buried truths to keep us company.

In this way, The Screaming Skull is more than a ghost story. It is a reckoning. A whisper turned into a scream. A quiet masterpiece of moral horror that still echoes more than a century after it was first told.

The Screaming Skull

I've heard it scream many times. I'm not jumpy or the type to make things up, and I never believed in ghosts—unless that thing counts as one. Whatever it is, it hates me, just like it hated Luke Pratt. And it screams at me.

If I were you, I wouldn't go around telling creepy stories about ways to kill people. You never know who's sitting at the table—someone might be sick of their spouse. I've always blamed myself for Mrs. Pratt's death. I didn't want anything bad to happen to her—really. But maybe if I hadn't told that story, she'd still be alive. That's probably why the thing screams at me.

She was kind, gentle, and always tried to keep the peace. I remember once she screamed when she thought her little boy had been shot by a pistol. Everyone knew it wasn't loaded, but she was terrified. That scream—it's the same one I hear now. High-pitched and shaky at the end. You'd know it if you heard it.

I didn't realize back then that she and the doctor weren't getting along. They argued sometimes when I was visiting. I saw her blush and bite her lip, trying not to snap, while Luke would go pale and say terrible things. He'd always been like that—even when we were kids. He was my cousin, which is how I ended up with this house. After he died and his son Charley was killed in South Africa, there weren't any family members left. It's a nice place, though—good for an old sailor like me who enjoys gardening now.

Funny how we remember our mistakes more clearly than anything else. I've thought about it a lot. One night, I was having dinner with the Pratts when I told them a story that changed everything. It was a cold, rainy night in November, and you could hear the ocean groaning outside. Wait—listen. You might hear it now.

There! Did you hear it? That's the tide. It's a gloomy sound, isn't it? You hear it most this time of year. Oh—there it is again! Don't be scared, it's just a noise. I'm glad you heard it, though. Some people say it's just the wind or my imagination. But it rarely happens more than once a night. Toss another log on the fire, and pour yourself another drink—yes, even if it's mostly water.

Do you remember old Blauklot, the carpenter from that German ship that saved us when the Clontarf sank? We were in the middle of a storm, far from any shore, and the ship rose and fell like clockwork. "Pity the poor folks ashore tonight, boys!" he shouted as he went off

14

to bed. I think of that a lot now that I've retired from the sea.

It was a night just like this. I was home for a bit, waiting to captain the Olympia on her first voyage—the one where she set the speed record. That was back in '92, early November.

The weather was terrible, Pratt was in a foul mood, and dinner was just awful—cold, undercooked, and barely edible. Poor Mrs. Pratt was so upset she made a Welsh rarebit at the table, hoping it would make up for everything. Maybe Luke had lost a patient that day. Whatever the reason, he was bitter.

"My wife is trying to poison me," he joked. "She'll succeed one day." She looked hurt. I laughed awkwardly and said she was too smart to try something so basic. Then I launched into stories about strange old murder methods—things like spun glass and chopped horsehair.

Luke was a doctor and knew way more than I did, but that only made me talk more. I told them about a woman in Ireland who got away with killing three husbands before anyone noticed. Ever hear that one? The fourth husband stayed awake, caught her in the act, and she was hanged. She used to drug them and pour melted lead into their ears while they slept.

No, that sound's just the wind shifting again. I can tell. The scream usually only comes once, even this time of year—when it all happened. Yes, it was November. Mrs. Pratt died suddenly not long after that dinner. I remember the date well because I got the news in New York after taking the Olympia out. You were on the Leofric that same year, right? I remember. Hard to believe how old we've gotten. Nearly fifty years since we were apprentices on the Clontarf. Remember Blauklot? "Pity the poor folks ashore!" Ha!

Have another sip. That's old Hulstkamp. I found it in the cellar when the house came to me. It's the same bottle I brought Luke from Amsterdam twenty-five years ago. He never touched a drop. Maybe he regrets that now.

Where was I? Oh, right—Mrs. Pratt's death. Luke must've been really lonely afterward. I visited him now and then. He always seemed tired, anxious. Said his medical work was getting to him, but he still refused to hire help. Time passed, and then his son died in South Africa. That really broke him. He still did his job well— no mistakes that anyone ever mentioned—but there was something off about him.

Luke had red hair and pale skin when he was young, and he was always thin. Later, his hair faded to a dull gray, and after his son died, he got so thin his head looked like a skull stretched tight with skin. His eyes were sharp and strange—unsettling.

He had a bulldog, Bumble, that Mrs. Pratt had loved. Sweetest dog you'd ever meet. He had a habit of curling his lip over a tooth that scared people, but he was harmless. In the evenings, Luke and Bumble would sit in silence, just staring at each other. That chair you're in now—that was hers. This one was Luke's. Bumble used to climb up by the footstool—he was too old to jump—and stare at Luke. Luke would stare back, looking more like a skull with glowing eyes every day.

After a few minutes, Bumble would start to shake all over, then suddenly let out this awful howl and bolt from the chair to hide under the sideboard, whimpering and making strange noises.

Honestly, considering how Luke looked, I don't blame the dog. I'm not the type to believe in spooky stuff, but I think someone really sensitive could've lost it around him. He looked terrifying.

Then, just before Christmas, I visited again. I was off work for a few weeks. Bumble wasn't around, so I asked casually if the old dog had passed.

"Yes," Luke said, with a strange tone. Then he paused and added, "I killed him. I couldn't take it anymore."

I asked why, even though I already knew.

"He'd sit in her chair, glare at me, and then start howling." Luke shivered. "He didn't suffer," he added quickly. "I gave him something to help him sleep, then used chloroform slowly. He wouldn't have felt a thing. It's been quieter since then."

I wasn't sure what he meant at first—it was like the words just slipped out of his mouth. But now I get it. He meant the screaming didn't happen as often once the dog was gone. Maybe at first he thought it was old Bumble howling in the yard at the moon. But that noise isn't anything like a dog's howl, is it?

Anyway, I know what it is—even if Luke didn't. It's just a sound. And a sound has never hurt anyone. But Luke had more imagination than I do. I'm sure there's something strange about this place, something I don't fully understand. Still, when I don't understand something, I call it a mystery—not a death sentence like Luke seemed to think it was.

Nobody understands everything—not you, not me, not even men who've sailed the world. Take tidal waves, for example. We used to just call them that, not knowing what caused them. Now we say they come from underwater earthquakes and have dozens of theories about how those work—though no one really knows.

Once, I got caught in a tidal wave at sea. A pen holder flew straight up from my desk and hit the ceiling. It happened to Captain Lecky too—he wrote about it in his book Wrinkles. If something like that happened in this room, a nervous person might call it ghosts or magic. But it's probably just a natural thing we haven't figured out yet. That's how I see it. Same with the voice or the scream—it's just a mystery, nothing more.

Now, what proof is there that Luke killed his wife? I wouldn't bring it up with anyone else, but since it's just you... All we really have is the fact that Mrs. Pratt died suddenly, just a few days after I told that creepy story at dinner. It could have been a coincidence. Lots of people die suddenly from heart problems. Luke called another doctor, and they both said it was her heart. Why not believe them?

Well, except for the ladle. I never told anyone about that. I found it in the bedroom cupboard, and it made me freeze. It was new—a small iron ladle, only used once or twice. Some melted lead was stuck to the bottom, gray with bits of hardened gunk. But that doesn't prove anything. Country doctors are usually handy guys. Maybe Luke used it to make a sinker for fishing or a weight for the clock. Still, when I saw it, it gave me a bad feeling. It looked too much like what I'd described in that murder story. You get what I mean? It gave me the creeps. I threw it into the sea, a mile from the Spit. It's probably rusted to nothing by now.

Luke must've bought it in the village years earlier. They still sell the same kind. Probably used for cooking. Still, it didn't need to be left where a curious maid could find it—with lead still inside. She might've told the other maid who heard my story. That second maid married a local plumber. She might remember it all.

You understand what I'm saying, right? Now that Luke is gone and buried next to his wife, I don't want to drag up anything that could ruin his name. They're both gone, and their son is too. Luke's death caused enough of a stir on its own.

What happened? He was found dead on the beach one morning, and they held an inquest. There were marks on his neck, but nothing had been stolen. The verdict was that he died "by the hands or teeth of someone or something unknown." Half the jury thought a large dog might've attacked him, even though there were no bite wounds.

Nobody knew when he'd gone out or where he'd been. He was found lying on his back above the high-tide line. Next to him was an old cardboard box that had belonged to his wife. The lid had fallen off. Inside was a skull—he seemed to be bringing it home. Doctors sometimes collect things like that. The skull had rolled out of the box and landed near his head. It was small, perfectly shaped, very white, and had a full set of upper teeth. But there was no lower jaw.

I found it here when I moved in. It was so clean and shiny, like it belonged in a glass display. The people here didn't know where it came from or what to do with it, so they put it back in the box and left it in the best bedroom's cupboard. Of course, they showed it to me when I arrived.

They also took me to the beach where Luke was found. An old fisherman showed me exactly how he had been lying and where the skull was. The only strange part was that the skull had rolled up the slope toward Luke's head instead of downhill. That didn't seem weird at the time, but I've thought about it a lot since then. The hill's steep. I'll take you there tomorrow if you want—I made a little pile of stones at the spot.

When he fell—or was pushed—the box hit the sand, popped open, and the skull rolled out. But instead of rolling down like it should have, it stopped right by his head, facing him. It took me a while to wonder about that. And when I did, I couldn't stop picturing it in my head.

You want to know what conclusion I came to? Well, I didn't figure out why the skull rolled that way. But I did get a terrible idea stuck in my head.

I'm not talking about ghosts or anything like that. Maybe they exist, maybe they don't. But I doubt ghosts can actually hurt you—just scare you. Personally, I'd rather face a ghost than a thick fog in the Channel with ships all around. No, what got to me was a simple idea. I don't know how it started, but once it did, I couldn't shake it.

One evening, sitting with a book and a pipe, I suddenly wondered if the skull might be Mrs. Pratt's. And I've never stopped wondering since. I know it sounds crazy—she had a proper burial and was laid to rest in the churchyard. It seems impossible that Luke would keep her skull in that box in their bedroom. But even though it goes against all logic, I still believe it. Doctors do strange things, things that seem creepy to regular folks like us.

And if it was her skull, then the only way Luke could've gotten it was by killing her, just like the woman in that story I told. Maybe he was afraid someone would dig up her body one day and find melted lead in her skull. That's how they caught the woman in my story— by finding the lead inside the skulls.

Luke must've remembered that detail. I don't want to think about what he did when it hit him. I've never liked horror stories, and I doubt you do either. But if you did, you might imagine the rest of the details I've tried to leave out.

It must've been awful. I see it all too clearly. I think he took the skull the night before the funeral, after the coffin was closed and the maid was asleep. He probably put something under the sheet to make it look like a head was still there. What do you think it was?

Yes, I know—I say I don't want to think about it, then go on describing everything like I was there. But I'm sure it was her sewing bag. I remember it clearly. She always used it in the evenings. It was made of soft brown fabric, and when it was full, it was about the right size… You get what I mean.

You can laugh at me, but you don't live here alone. You didn't tell Luke the story about the melted lead. I'm not nervous, but sometimes I understand why people are. I think about all this when I'm alone. I dream about it. And when that thing screams—well, I still hate the sound, even though I should be used to it by now.

I really shouldn't be nervous. I've been on a haunted ship. We had a ghost in the mast, and two-thirds of the crew died of fever within ten days. But I was fine. I've seen worse than most. Yet nothing ever stuck with me like this.

I've tried to get rid of the skull, but it won't have it. It wants to stay—in Mrs. Pratt's old box, in the cupboard of the best bedroom. Nowhere else. How do I know that? Because I've tried to move it. You didn't think I hadn't tried, did you?

As long as it's here, the screaming only happens now and then—usually around this time of year. But when I take it out of the house, the screaming goes on all night. No servant has ever stayed a full day after that. I've often been left alone, managing the place myself for weeks. Nobody in the village will stay the night here anymore. Selling or renting it is out of the question.

The old women say that if I keep living here, I'll come to a bad end too.

I wasn't scared by it. You're smiling now, probably thinking it's silly that anyone would believe something so strange. And honestly, I agree—it sounds like complete nonsense. I even said it was just a sound, remember? Back when you jumped and looked around like you expected to see a ghost behind your chair?

Maybe I'm wrong about the skull. I actually hope I am—at least when I can convince myself of it. Maybe it really is just an old skull Luke found years ago. That rattling sound inside when you shake it could be anything—maybe a small rock or a piece of dried clay. Old skulls often have bits of stuff inside them. No, I've never tried to take it out. I'm afraid it might be lead, you see. And if it is lead… then I'd feel just as guilty as if I had done the killing myself. I think anyone would understand that.

But since I don't know for sure, I can at least pretend it's all just a silly story. I can tell myself that Mrs. Pratt died of natural causes, and that the skull was just something Luke had from his student days in London. But if I knew it was lead, I think I'd have to leave this house. Honestly, I do. As it is, I had to stop sleeping in the best bedroom—the one with the cupboard.

You ask why I don't just throw the thing in the pond? I could, but please don't call it a "confounded bugbear." It doesn't like being called names.

There! Hear that scream? I told you! You're looking pale now. Sit closer to the fire. Fill up your pipe again and have another drink. This old Hollands liquor won't hurt you. I saw a Dutchman drink half a jug of the stuff in Java once and it didn't even faze him. I don't drink rum myself—it makes my joints ache—but it won't bother you. And it's a damp night. Listen to that wind howl. The windows are rattling. The tide must have turned too—do you hear that long moaning sound?

I don't think we would've heard the scream again if you hadn't called it a name. Really. Oh, sure, you can say it was just a coincidence if you want. But please don't insult the thing again. Maybe Mrs. Pratt hears it, and maybe it upsets her. Who knows?

Ghost? No, I wouldn't call it that. You can pick it up and look at it in the daylight. You can even shake it and hear it rattle. That's not what most people think of when they say "ghost." But whatever it is, it can hear—and understand. I'm sure of that.

When I first moved in, I tried sleeping in the best bedroom because it was the nicest. But it used to be their room—Luke and Mrs. Pratt's. The big bed where she died is still there, and the cupboard is built into the wall, right by the headboard on the left. That's where it wants to stay, in the box. I lasted about two weeks in that room before I gave up and moved downstairs into the little room next to the old doctor's office. Luke used to sleep there when he thought he might be called out at night.

I've always been a solid sleeper on land. I usually sleep from eleven to seven, or from midnight to eight if someone's visiting. But in that bedroom, I couldn't sleep past three in the morning—more exactly, seventeen minutes past three. I even timed it with my old pocket watch. It never changed. I wonder if that's the time she died.

It wasn't like the scream you just heard. If it had been, I couldn't have stayed even one more night. It was more like a quick gasp, a soft moan, and some strange breathing sounds coming from the cupboard. The kind of noise that would never normally wake anyone up. But I always woke up from it.

You probably know what I mean—people like us, who've been at sea, don't wake up for normal noises. You could sleep through the loudest storm if it's just wind and waves. But if something small, like a pencil, rolls around in a drawer, you're up in a second. That's what this was like—small, but strange enough to wake me instantly.

When I say it was like a "start," I mean the kind of tiny sound you might hear when someone suddenly moves a little—like a quick breath or the faint rustle of clothing. You don't hear it, exactly, but you feel it. You just know something moved. It reminded me of steering a ship. Before a ship shifts, you can feel it a second or two ahead of time through the wheel. Riders say the same thing about horses. It's like an instinct. And I think a ship's like that—it feels alive and passes on its feelings to the person steering it.

Anyway, that's how I felt in that room. I sensed something moving in the cupboard. I felt it so clearly that it woke me, even though there might not have been a real sound at all. But then there was a sound—quiet, like it was coming from far away through a phone, but I knew it was right there, in the cupboard near the head of my bed.

It didn't scare me at first. My hair didn't stand up. My blood didn't freeze. I was just annoyed, like I would've been if a drawer started rattling while I was trying to sleep. I thought maybe wind was blowing through a crack in the cupboard. So I lit a candle, checked the time—it was seventeen minutes past three—and rolled over to sleep on my right side. That's my good ear. I'm half-deaf in the other one from a fall when I was a kid. I dove from a ship's rigging and hit the water wrong. A stupid stunt, but the hearing loss is useful now—I can sleep through anything when I lie on that side.

The same thing happened again a few times, always at exactly the same time. But not every night—maybe because I wasn't always sleeping on my good ear. I checked the cupboard. It was sealed tight—no drafts, no cracks. I figured Mrs. Pratt used to store her winter clothes in there. It still smelled like camphor and turpentine.

After a couple of weeks, I'd had enough. Up to that point, I kept telling myself not to be silly, that it would look different in the morning. But the sound got louder. One night, I even heard it in my bad ear. That's how I knew it wasn't just in my head—I had my good ear buried in the pillow, so I shouldn't have heard anything. But I did.

I don't know if it scared me or just made me mad. Sometimes those two feelings feel the same. Either way, I snapped. I lit a candle, jumped out of bed, opened the cupboard, grabbed the box, and threw it out the window—just as far as I could.

That's when I felt the hair on my neck stand up. The thing let out a high, sharp scream, like a bomb flying through the air. It landed somewhere beyond the road. The night was pitch black, so I couldn't see it hit the ground, but I was sure it had flown over the fence and across the road. My window is right above the front door—it's about fifteen yards to the fence and another ten yards across the road. Beyond that, there's a thick hedge along the vicarage land.

I didn't get much sleep after that. About half an hour later, I heard another scream outside. It sounded like the one we heard tonight—only worse. It was filled with sadness and despair. Maybe it was just my imagination, but I could've sworn the cries were getting closer each time. I lit my pipe and paced around the room, then tried reading to distract myself. But I couldn't focus. I don't remember what the book was or what it said. That awful sound kept pulling me back, like it wanted to wake the dead.

Just before sunrise, I heard someone knock at the front door. This was different—it was a real knock, not like the screams. I opened my window and looked down. I figured someone needed a doctor and didn't realize Luke no longer lived here. After all that creepy noise, it was actually kind of nice to hear something normal.

I couldn't see the doorstep from above because of the porch roof. The knock came again. I shouted, asking who was there. No one answered, but the knocking didn't stop. I yelled once more, telling them the doctor didn't live here anymore. Still nothing. Then I thought, maybe it was an old man who couldn't hear me. So I grabbed a candle and headed downstairs.

Honestly, I wasn't even thinking about the skull at that point. I had nearly forgotten the screams. I just assumed someone was at the door with a message. I set the candle down on the hallway table so the wind wouldn't blow it out. As I slid back the bolt, I heard the knock again—soft this time, with a hollow kind of echo. But I still thought it was just someone outside.

It wasn't. No one was there. But just as I opened the door and stepped to the side to peek out, something rolled over the doorstep and hit my foot.

I jumped back the second I felt it. I didn't need to look—I already knew what it was. I can't explain how, but I just knew. And it didn't make sense. I was sure I had thrown it over the road. The window I'd tossed it from opens wide, and I'd given it a good throw. Later that morning, I found the box exactly where I thought it would be—past the hedge.

Maybe you think the box popped open midair and the skull fell out—but that's impossible. You can't throw an empty cardboard box that far. Try tossing a crumpled paper ball or an eggshell. It just doesn't work.

Anyway, I shut and locked the door, picked the skull up carefully, and placed it on the table beside the candle.

I did it without even thinking—like how you act on instinct during something scary. My first thought, oddly enough, was that someone might come by and find me standing there, the skull by my foot, as if it were blaming me. As it sat on the table, the candlelight flickered across its empty eye sockets, making them look like they were opening and closing.

Then, out of nowhere, the candle went out. The door was shut, there was no draft. I used up half a box of matches trying to relight it.

I sank into a chair without even realizing why. I think I was just badly shaken—and who wouldn't be? That thing had come back. It wanted to be inside again. I stared at it until I started feeling cold, then picked it up, carried it upstairs, and put it back where it belonged. I even remember talking to it, promising I'd return its box in the morning.

You want to know if I stayed in the room? I did, but I kept the light on all night. I smoked and read—not because I was brave, but because I was scared. It was fear, plain and simple. Not cowardice, just fear. I couldn't have stayed in that room with the skull in the dark cupboard. That thing had crossed the road by itself, climbed the stairs, and knocked to come back in.

When the sun came up, I put on my boots and went outside to find the box. I had to take the long way around, through the gate by the road. I found the bandbox hanging in the hedge, caught by the string. The lid had fallen off and was lying on the ground. That proves it didn't open midair. The skull must have traveled with it across the road.

That's everything. I took the box back upstairs, put the skull inside, and locked the cupboard. When the maid brought me breakfast, she told me she was quitting. Didn't care about her pay—she just wanted to leave. Her face looked sickly and pale. I acted surprised and asked what was wrong. But she didn't want to explain. She just asked me how I could stay in a haunted house, and if I really thought I'd survive much longer. She said she might've believed I was a little deaf, but even I couldn't sleep through screams like that. And if I had slept through it, why had I been walking around and opening the front door in the middle of the night?

I couldn't argue—she'd heard me. So she left. Later that morning, I went into the village and found another woman to do the cleaning and cooking. But she only agreed if she could go home every night. That same day, I moved out of the best bedroom and I haven't been back since.

After a while, I hired two older sisters from London. They were tough Scotswomen, very practical. I warned them the house made strange noises and had a creepy reputation in the village. I said the locals liked ghost stories. They just rolled their eyes and said Cornish ghosts didn't scare them. They'd worked in two haunted houses before and had never seen anything—not even the "Boy in Gray," which they said was no big deal back in Forfarshire.

They lived with me for a few months, and while they were here, everything was calm. One of the sisters came back later, but both of them had left before the year was up. The one who returned—she used to be the cook—ended up marrying the sexton, the man who helps me with the garden now. It worked out well. This is a small village, and he didn't have much to do before. He's good with plants and handles the heavier tasks, which is helpful since I'm not as young and flexible as I once was. He's quiet, keeps to himself, and was already a widower when I moved in. His name is James Trehearn.

The sisters never said anything strange about the house, but when November came, they gave notice. They said the chapel was too far away in the next parish, and they didn't want to go to our local church. Still, the younger one came back in the spring, and as soon as they could post the banns, she married James. Since then, she hasn't had any trouble hearing him preach. That's fine with me. If she's happy, I'm happy. They live in a small cottage that looks out over the churchyard.

You might be wondering why I'm telling you all this. I admit, I do tend to talk a lot when I finally have company—it's just nice to have someone to talk to. But in this case, it matters. You see, James Trehearn was the one who buried Mrs. Pratt and later her husband, both in the same grave. That grave is just behind his cottage. That's why I think of it so often. I get the feeling he knows more than he lets on. He doesn't talk much, but you can tell something's on his mind.

Now I stay in the house alone at night. Mrs. Trehearn handles all the housework during the day, and when I have a guest, James's niece helps serve meals. In winter, he walks his wife home every evening. In summer, she goes alone while there's still light. She's a brave woman, but she's not quite as sure as she used to be that Scotland is the only place with ghosts. Funny how some Scots act like the supernatural is a local specialty. It's a strange kind of national pride, don't you think?

That fire's burning nicely, isn't it? There's nothing like driftwood once it catches. We get plenty of it here, though it's a shame—it means shipwrecks still happen along this lonely coast. Trehearn and I take a cart now and then and pick some up near the Spit. I prefer a wood fire over coal any day. Even a chunk of an old ship beam feels like company when it burns. The salt in the wood makes the sparks fly like little fireworks. Look at that! Makes it easy to forget about the thing upstairs—at least while the wind is quiet. It'll blow again before morning, though. Just a pause for now.

You want to see the skull? I don't mind. Take a look. It's nearly perfect, except for two missing front teeth in the lower jaw.

Oh—that reminds me. I didn't tell you about the jaw yet. Trehearn found it last spring while digging a pit for a new asparagus bed. You know how deep those need to be—six or eight feet. If you ever want one dug right, get a sexton. They're experts at digging.

He had gone down about three feet when he hit a layer of white lime on one side of the trench. He noticed the soil was looser there, but said it hadn't been disturbed in years. He probably thought lime wouldn't be good for the plants, so he scooped it out and tossed it aside. It was packed hard, and out of habit, he broke it up with his spade. That's when the jawbone fell out. He figured he must've knocked out the two front teeth when he hit it, but he never found them.

Trehearn has handled things like this before, so he said right away it likely belonged to a young woman. The teeth must have been complete when she died. He brought it to me and asked if I wanted to keep it. If not, he said he'd bury it properly in the next grave he dug, since it probably belonged to a Christian and should be laid to rest. I told him doctors sometimes use quicklime to clean bones, and maybe Dr. Pratt had a lime pit in the garden for that and just forgot about the jaw.

Trehearn just gave me a quiet look.

"Maybe it belonged to the skull that used to be in the cupboard upstairs," he said. "Maybe Dr. Pratt put the skull in the lime to clean it, and when he took it out, he left the lower jaw behind. There's some human hair stuck in the lime too, sir."

I saw that there was, just like Trehearn said. If he didn't suspect anything, why would he even suggest the jaw might match the skull? And it did. That proves he knows more than he lets on. Do you think he looked at the body before she was buried? Or maybe—when he buried Luke in the same grave...

Well, no point digging that up again, right? I told him I'd keep the jaw with the skull. I took it upstairs and placed it where it belonged. There's no doubt the two go together. Now they're back in the same box.

Trehearn knows a lot. One time we were talking about fixing the kitchen walls, and he casually mentioned that it hadn't been done since the week Mrs. Pratt died. He didn't say it directly, but he probably figured the lime he found in the garden came from that same job. He's one of those quiet types who sees everything and puts the pieces together in his head. And since the grave is just behind his cottage, and he's one of the fastest diggers I've ever seen, he could find out the truth if he wanted. No one in this quiet little village would ever know—unless he decided to tell.

The scariest part is thinking about how calm Luke must've been if he really did it. He must've been so sure he'd never be caught. His nerves must have been like steel. Sometimes I feel like it's hard enough just living in this house—where it might have happened. I always say if it happened. I do it to protect Luke's memory... and maybe to protect my own peace of mind too.

I'll go get the box in a minute. Let me light my pipe first—no need to rush! We had supper early, and it's only half-past nine. I never let a guest go to bed before midnight, or without at least three glasses. You can have more if you want—but never less. That's tradition.

Listen to that wind picking up again. It was only calm for a bit—we're in for a wild night.

Something strange happened when I fit the jaw to the skull. I'm not usually jumpy, but it startled me. You know how sometimes you think you're alone, and someone appears suddenly behind you? You flinch— not because you're scared, but just out of shock. That's what it was like.

When I placed the jaw under the skull, the teeth snapped shut on my finger. It felt like it actually bit me! I jumped, and then realized I had been pressing the two pieces together with my other hand. It gave me a shock, that's all. It was bright daylight, and the sun was pouring into the bedroom. It would've been silly to be scared... but even so, it made me feel uneasy.

It reminded me of the coroner's strange verdict about Luke's death: "by the hand or teeth of some person or animal unknown." Since then, I've often wished I'd seen those marks on his neck—though the lower jaw was missing back then.

People do odd things without realizing it. I once saw a man hanging over the edge of a ship, holding on with one hand, and he was just about to cut the rope he was gripping—with a knife in his other hand! He had no idea what he was doing. I think that's how it was when I got my finger caught. Still, it felt so real, like the thing was alive and wanted to bite me. And honestly, I believe it hates me. Poor thing.

Do you think the thing that rattles inside it might be lead? I'll bring the box down in a bit. If it falls into your hand, that's your problem! If it's just a bit of dirt or a stone, I'll be relieved—and I'll probably stop thinking about the skull for good. But I can't bring myself to shake it out and check. Just the idea that it might be lead really bothers me. Still... I know I'll find out soon. I just know it. And I'm sure Trehearn already knows, though he keeps quiet.

All right, I'll go get it now. What's that? You want to come with me? Ha! You think I'm scared of a box and a noise? That's nonsense!

Ugh, the candle won't light. It's like the stupid thing knows what it's for! That's the third match already. They light fine for my pipe. Look, it's a new box, straight from the tin I keep sealed up because of the damp.

You think maybe the candle's wick is damp? Maybe. I'll just light it in the fireplace—that always works. It's sputtering a bit, but it's lit now. Just like any other candle, really. Still, candles around here aren't great. I don't know where they're made, but sometimes they burn low with a weird greenish flame and spit tiny sparks. They even go out for no reason. That's just how it is. It'll be a long time before our village gets electric lights.

Not a great light, is it?

You think I should leave you the candle and take the lamp? I don't like carrying lamps. I've never dropped one, but I always worry I will, and that's dangerous. Plus, I've gotten used to these crummy candles.

Go ahead and finish your drink while I get the box. You're not getting out of having three glasses, you know. And you won't have to sleep upstairs—I've put you in the old study next to the surgery. That's where I stay now. I don't ask anyone to sleep upstairs anymore. The last person who did was Crackenthorpe, and he said he didn't sleep a wink.

You remember Crack, right? He stayed in the Service and just made admiral. Who would've thought the skinny little kid he used to be would go the farthest? If anyone had told us that back then, we'd have laughed!

Anyway, you and I did pretty well ourselves. I'm going now. Don't think I'm stalling by talking so much. I'm not afraid. And if I was afraid, I'd say so—and I'd ask you to come with me!

*****

Here's the box. I carried it down very carefully so I wouldn't shake it too much. If it got jostled, the jaw might fall off again—and I don't think it would like that. Yes, the candle went out on the stairs, but that was just the draft from the broken window. Did you hear something? Yeah, there was another scream. You think I look pale? It's nothing—my heart sometimes acts up, and I took the stairs too fast. That's one reason I prefer living on the ground floor now.

Whatever made that noise, it wasn't the skull. I had the box in my hands when it happened. So that proves it must be coming from somewhere else. I'm sure I'll figure it out someday—probably just a hole in the wall, or a loose window frame. That's how ghost stories usually end. I'm glad I brought the box down for you to see, though. That scream proves the skull didn't make it. Imagine thinking a skull could scream like a real person!

Now I'll open the box so we can take a good look in the light. It's strange to think that Mrs. Pratt used to sit in that very chair, in this same light, night after night. But I've decided the whole thing is nonsense. It's just an old skull Luke kept from when he studied medicine. Maybe he used the lime to clean it and just forgot the jaw.

See this? I sealed the string after I put the jaw back, and I even wrote on the box lid. The original label is still there, from when the hat was delivered to Mrs. Pratt. Since there was space, I added, "A skull, once the property of the late Luke Pratt, M.D." Not sure why— maybe just to explain why I had it. Sometimes I wonder what kind of hat came in this box. Maybe something bright and cheerful, with feathers and ribbons. Funny to think this box might've once held a hat… and now, maybe the head that wore it. But no, we agreed it probably came from the hospital where Luke studied. That's a better explanation. It's easier to believe it has nothing to do with Mrs. Pratt or my old story about the lead.

Wait—what was that? Quick—grab the lamp! Don't let it go out! I'll shut the window—it's blowing like crazy! Great, now the lamp's out too. At least we still have the fire. Okay, I got the window shut. The bolt wasn't all the way down before. Did the box fall? Where is it? There—we're safe now. I used the old wooden bar on the window. Those old bars still work great. Now help me find the box while I relight the lamp. These matches are useless—yes, a bit of paper works better. Thanks. Got it! Okay, now put the box back on the table and we'll open it.

That's the first time I've ever seen the wind burst that window open. Part of it was my fault—I didn't close it right. Yes, I heard the scream. It seemed to circle the house and then come through the window. That proves it's just the wind. Or my imagination. I guess I'm more imaginative than I thought. Funny how we get to know ourselves better as we grow older.

I think I'll have a sip of that Hulstkamp, just this once. Since you're having another glass, I might as well join you. That cold wind hit hard, and with my stiff joints, I don't want to catch a chill. Once it gets in, it stays all winter.

Wow—that's strong! Let me light a new pipe now that everything's calm again. I'm really glad we heard that last scream together—while the skull was right here. That proves it couldn't have been the skull making the sound. You thought it screamed through the room when the window flew open? So did I—but it must've just been the wind. What else could it be?

Look at this—I want you to see that the wax seal is still intact before we open it. Need my glasses? No? Okay. You can read the motto—"Sweet and low." That's from the poem, you know? "Wind of the western sea…" and all that. My wife gave me this seal when we were dating, and I've always kept it on my watch chain. She loved Tennyson.

No need to cut the string—it's tied to the box. I'll just break the wax and undo the knot. Then we'll reseal it afterward. I like knowing it's secure, and that no one has tampered with it. Not that I'd suspect Trehearn, but I still think he knows more than he says.

There—we're in. I didn't have to break the string, either. I didn't think I'd ever open this box again, honestly. The lid comes off easily. Okay... take a look.

What? It's empty?

There's nothing in it?

The skull is gone!

*****

No, there's nothing wrong with me. I'm just trying to get my thoughts together. It's all so strange. I'm absolutely sure the skull was inside the box when I sealed it last spring. There's no way I imagined that. If I was someone who drank too much, I might think I made some silly mistake—but I'm not. I never did. The most I ever had was a pint of beer with dinner and a little rum before bed. Funny how it's always the people who don't drink much that end up with aches and pains.

Still, there's the seal I made, and here's the box—completely empty. That much is clear.

Honestly, I don't like this one bit. Something's not right. Don't start talking to me about ghosts or supernatural stuff, because I don't believe in any of that. Someone must have broken the seal and taken the skull. I sometimes leave my watch and chain on the table when I go work in the garden. Maybe Trehearn took the seal then. He would've known I'd be outside for a while.

If it wasn't him—don't even suggest the skull moved on its own! If it did, then it has to be somewhere in the house. Maybe hiding in some dark corner, just waiting. It could be anywhere. And when we find it, it'll scream again—it always screams at me. It hates me. I know it does.

Look—the box is completely empty. We're both awake and clear-headed. I'll even turn it upside down. Wait—did you hear that? Something fell out. It's on the floor—by your feet, I think. Help me find it. Did you get it? Please, hand it to me—quick!

Lead. I knew it the moment I heard it hit the floor. Nothing else would make that dull thump on the rug. So it really was lead. That means Luke did it.

I'm a little shaken—not scared exactly, just really unsettled. Anyone would be, I think. And it's not like I was afraid to bring the box down—I thought the skull was still inside. That takes guts, right? I'll even carry it back upstairs and put it in the cupboard again if I have to. It's not fear—it's the awful feeling that I helped cause her death. That poor woman. All because I told that story. That's what really gets to me. Deep down, I hoped I'd never know for sure, but now I do. Look at this.

Look at it—that tiny lump of lead. It's nothing special to look at, but just imagine what it did. Doesn't it make your skin crawl? He must've given her something to knock her out first. But there must've been a moment—just one—where she felt it. Can you imagine someone pouring boiling lead into your brain? She died before she could even scream... but still, just thinking about it—

There! That sound again! It's outside—I know it is. I can't get it out of my head!

You thought I passed out? I wish I had—it would've stopped the sound. You say it's just noise, that noise can't hurt anyone—well, look at yourself. You're pale too. There's only one thing we can do if we want to sleep tonight. We have to find the skull and put it back in the box. Then we'll lock it in the cupboard—where it wants to be. I don't know how it got out, but it's trying to return. That's why the screams are worse than ever tonight. It's never been this bad—not since the beginning.

Bury it? Sure, if we find it, we'll bury it. Even if we're up all night. We'll dig six feet down, pack the dirt tight, so it can't get out again. If it still screams, at least we won't hear it down there. Let's grab the lantern and start searching. It can't be far. I'm sure it was just about to come in when I shut the window.

You're right. I need to pull myself together. Don't say anything for a moment—I'll sit quietly with my eyes closed and repeat something I know by heart. That usually helps.

"Add the altitude, latitude, and polar distance. Divide by two and subtract the altitude from the half-sum. Then add the log of the secant of the latitude, the cosecant of the polar distance, the cosine of the half-sum, and the sine of the half-sum minus the altitude."

There. Don't say I've lost my mind—my memory's working fine, isn't it?

Of course, you might say that's just habit—something I've used all my life. But that's the point. When someone's losing their mind, it's the automatic stuff that breaks first. They remember things that never happened. They see things that aren't there. They hear sounds in silence. That's not what's happening to us, right?

Come on. Let's get the lantern and check around the house. It's not raining—just windy. You remember where the lantern is? In the cupboard under the stairs. I always keep it ready, just in case there's a shipwreck.

You say there's no use looking for it? I don't agree. And forget what I said earlier about burying it—it doesn't want to be buried. It wants to be back in the bandbox and taken upstairs. Trehearn must've taken it, I'm sure. Maybe he tried to do the right thing. Maybe he thought if he buried it properly in the churchyard, it would stop screaming. Maybe he meant well.

It sounds reasonable, right? He figured it was screaming because it hadn't been buried with the rest. But he was wrong. It's screaming because it hates me— because I'm the reason that little piece of lead was ever used.

Still think we shouldn't look for it? That's nonsense. It wants us to find it.

Wait—listen! Do you hear that knocking? Three times—then a pause—then again. It sounds hollow, doesn't it?

It's back. I've heard that knock before. It wants to come in. It wants to be taken back upstairs, into its box.

Will you come with me? We'll bring it in together. I'll admit it—I don't want to go alone. I know it'll roll across the floor and stop against my foot—just like last time. And then the light will go out. I'm already shaken from finding the lead, and my heart isn't what it used to be—too much strong tobacco, maybe. But yeah, I'm nervous tonight. I'll admit that.

Good—come on. I'll bring the box so I don't have to come back again. Do you hear the knocking? It's not like any normal knock. If you'll hold the door open, I can grab the lantern from under the stairs using just the light from this room. No need to bring the lamp—it'll just blow out again.

It knows we're coming—listen! It's eager to get inside. Don't close the door until the lantern is ready, no matter what. Usually the matches give me trouble— but look, the first one worked! That's proof enough it wants in—no trouble at all. Okay, shut the door now, please. Now come help me with the lantern. It's so windy out there I'll need both hands. Hold the light low. Can you still hear the knocking? Here we go—I'll open the door just a little with my foot braced at the bottom—now!

Grab it! It's just the wind blowing it across the floor—there's a full-blown storm outside, I'm telling you! Got it? Good. The bandbox is on the table now. Just a second while I put the bar back in place. Done!

Why did you toss it into the box so roughly? It doesn't like that, you know.

What's that? It bit your hand? Don't be ridiculous! You did exactly what I did before. You pressed the jaw shut with your other hand and pinched yourself. Let me see. You're bleeding? You must've pressed really hard—look at that, the skin's torn. I'll get you some antiseptic before bed. People say a scratch from a skull's tooth can cause trouble.

Come back in and let me see it better by the lamp. I'll bring the bandbox—no need for the lantern, just leave it burning in the hall. I'll need it again when I go back upstairs. Go ahead and close the door if you want—it's cozier that way. Is your finger still bleeding? I'll grab the carbolic solution. Just let me have a look.

Yuck! There's a drop of blood on the upper jaw— right on the eye tooth. Creepy, isn't it? When I saw it sliding across the floor in the hall, I almost lost my grip. My knees felt weak. Then I realized it was just the wind pushing it across the boards. You don't blame me, do you? Of course not. We've known each other since we were kids, and we've both been through plenty. Let's be honest—we were both scared out of our minds when that thing came at you across the floor. No wonder you hurt your hand picking it up—especially after that. I did the same thing in broad daylight, with the sun shining in the room.

Strange how tightly the jaw sticks now, isn't it? Must be the damp air—it clamps shut like a vice. I wiped off the blood. It wasn't a nice sight. Don't worry, I'm not going to mess with it or try opening it. I won't play tricks on it. I'm just going to reseal the box and take it back upstairs where it belongs. The sealing wax is on the writing table by the window. Thanks. I won't be leaving my seal lying around again, not with Trehearn in the house.

Explain it? I'm not trying to explain anything weird. But if you want to believe Trehearn hid it in the bushes and the wind blew it to the door—enough to make it knock—I won't say that's impossible. I'm happy to agree if it makes sense to you.

Here—look at this. You've seen me seal it this time. So if something happens again, you'll know I did it. The wax holds the strings to the lid so it can't be opened at all—not even a crack. You believe me, don't you? Good.

And from now on, I'm keeping the cupboard locked and the key in my pocket.

Alright, let's take the lantern and go upstairs. Honestly, I'm starting to believe your idea that the wind blew it in. I'll go first, since I know the stairs. Just keep the lantern low so I can see my feet. Listen to that wind howl! Did you feel the sand on the floor as we crossed the hall?

Here we are—this is the best bedroom. Hold up the lantern, please. Over here, near the head of the bed. I left the cupboard open when I came down with the box. Isn't it strange how the smell of a woman's clothes can stay in an old closet for years?

This is the shelf. You've seen me put the box back. And now, you see me lock the cupboard. And here— I'm putting the key in my pocket. That's done.

*****

Good night. Are you sure you're comfortable enough? It's not the nicest room, but I figure you'd rather sleep here than upstairs tonight. If you need anything, just call out—there's only a thin wall between our rooms. The wind isn't nearly as loud on this side of the house. There's some Hollands on the table if you want one last drink before bed. No? That's fine, up to you. Good night again—and try not to dream about that thing, if you can help it.

*****

The following paragraph appeared in the Penraddon News, 23rd November, 1906:

"MYSTERIOUS DEATH OF A RETIRED SEA CAPTAIN

The village of Tredcombe is very shaken by the strange and mysterious death of Captain Charles Braddock. People are spreading all kinds of unbelievable stories, since what actually happened is hard to explain. Captain Braddock, who had once been in charge of the biggest and fastest ships of a major transatlantic company, was found dead in his bed on Tuesday morning. He lived alone in a small cottage about a quarter mile from the village.

The local doctor examined the body and found something horrifying: the captain had been bitten in the throat by a person with such force that his windpipe was crushed, causing his death. The bite marks were so clear that every tooth could be counted—except for the two middle teeth on the bottom, which were missing. Investigators hope this detail might help identify who did it. They believe the killer is a dangerous escaped mental patient.

It's especially strange because Captain Braddock was strong and healthy for his age—over sixty-five—and there were no signs of a struggle in the room. It's also unclear how anyone could've gotten inside the house. Warnings have been sent out to mental hospitals across the country, but so far, there's been no word about any missing patients.

The jury in the coroner's inquest gave a very unusual decision: they said Captain Braddock died "by the hands or teeth of some person unknown." The village doctor has quietly said he thinks the attacker might have been a woman, based on how small the bite marks are.

The whole case remains a mystery. Captain Braddock was a widower, lived by himself, and had no children.

(Note: People interested in ghost stories and haunted places might recognize that this tale is based on legends about a skull kept at a farmhouse called Bettiscombe Manor, which is believed to be on the coast of Dorset.)

The End

Thank You for Reading

Dear Reader,

We hope this timeless classic has sparked your imagination and enriched your literary journey. Now that you've turned the final page, we want to share a vision for the future of reading—one where every classic you've ever wanted to explore is at your fingertips, in a format that best suits your life.

We'd like to invite you to gain immediate, unlimited digital & audiobook access to hundreds of the most treasured literary classics ever written—along with the option to secure deluxe paperback, hardcover & box set editions at printing cost. Together, we can spark a new global literary renaissance alongside our small, independent publishing house called "The Library of Alexandria."

Thousands of years ago, the Library of Alexandria stood as a beacon of knowledge—until it was lost to history. We aim to reignite that spirit of preservation and discovery right now, in the modern age—only this time, it's accessible to all, in every language and every format.

Picture a world where every timeless classic, novel, poem, or philosophical treatise is not only available to read but also updated for today's readers—modernized, translated into any language or dialect, and ready to enjoy in any format you choose, whether that is in an eBook, audiobook, paperback, or deluxe hardcover & box set version a printing cost.

By joining our movement to rebuild the modern Library of Alexandria, you become part of an unprecedented mission to offer:

- **Unlimited Audiobook & eBook Access to the Greatest Classics of All Time**

  Instantly explore thousands of legendary works, from Plato and Shakespeare to Jane Austen and Leo Tolstoy. All are instantly ready to read or listen to, giving you a complete literary universe at your fingertips.

- **Paperback & Deluxe Editions at Printing Costs:**

  Purchase any title in a paperback, deluxe hardbound, or deluxe boxset edition at printing costs, shipped right to your doorstep. Curate your personal library of Alexandria with editions worthy of display— crafted to last, designed to captivate, and delivered straight to your door.

- **Modern translations for Contemporary Readers in all languages and dialects**

  Discover a vast selection of classics reimagined in clear, current language—no more struggling with outdated phrases or obscure references. Next to the original versions, we aim to offer translations in as many languages and dialects as possible.

  As we continue our translation efforts and add new languages, readers everywhere can connect with these works as if they were written today. By bridging linguistic divides, you're contributing to ensuring that these timeless stories become more meaningful, accessible, and inspiring for people across the globe.

- **Your Personal Library of Alexandria:**

  Over the months and years, you'll curate a unique physical archive of classics—each volume a testament to your taste, curiosity, and love of knowledge. It's not just about owning books—it's about curating a cultural legacy you'll cherish and pass down for generations to come.

- **Join a Global Literary Renaissance:**

  Your support fuels an ongoing mission: allowing us to reinvest in offering deluxe print editions (including special boxsets) at their true cost, broaden the range of available formats and translations, and extend the reach of these works to new audiences worldwide. By joining today, you're not just preserving a legacy of masterpieces; you set in motion a powerful wave of literary accessibility.

We are more than a publisher—we're a movement, and we can't do it alone. Your support lets us scale our mission, preserving and reimagining history's greatest works for tomorrow's readers.

Become a Torchbearer of knowledge.

Thank you for picking up this book and allowing us into your literary journey. As you turn the pages, know that you're part of something larger: a global effort to keep these stories alive, share their wisdom across borders and generations, and spark a true cultural revival for the modern era.

If this resonates with you—please consider taking the next step by visiting:

www.libraryofalexandria.com

With gratitude and a shared love of knowledge,

The Modern Library of Alexandria Team

Visit:

www.libraryofalexandria.com

Or scan the code below: